Carey Harris

CAREY FINDING CAREY

Carey Harris

620 McCarthy Way

Los Angeles CA 90019

www.snhpr.com

ISBN: 978-1-7325543-6-8

Table of Contents

CHAPTER 1

HE'S ON HIS WAY

Growing up in an urban setting was especially hard for 16-year old Carey because he'd been nurturing big dreams since he was a child and didn't see the possibility of any of them coming true in the neighborhood he was growing up in. Living in a city was supposed to be full of opportunities, but for Carey he often felt sheltered; trapped; as though the walls that were supposed to keep him safe were locking him in.

It wasn't all bad. There was a lot about the place he did like; it's just that his dreams were taking him somewhere else – and he had already decided to do something about it.

Carey always had a vivid imagination. As he walked past the dirty, graffiti covered walls he found patterns in the artist's squiggles. He could make images out of anything and find beauty in the darkest places. As he wandered by, the paint seemed to move by itself and he picked out words in his mind. The colors swirled and twirled across the wall and as words popped out, he felt a song forming in his mind.

"Dance away to the big wide world out there,

You could be living free without a care.

You deserve better than this dirty town,

If you stay here you'll lose your smile to a frown.

Go Carey, dream big and wide,

There's a world waiting for you right outside.

Play with your friends and have a great day,

But tomorrow you must dream bigger and get away!"

He hummed the tune of the song he had made to himself as he continued to make his way along the street. The clusters of squashed chewing gum mixed with rain water to make the most curious patterns. The city was dingy and rough but the people there were pure and genuine. It was a good community to live in.

Carey felt lucky to live in a town like this; where everyone was friendly. People spoke to their neighbors: unlike in some of the bigger cities, this small town had a sense of community. He had a great family too. His parents were still together: they had been married for twenty years and were still as happy as the day they had met. At least that was what Carey assumed.

The town was great and his family was perfect. They even had a dog named Jackson who had become like a brother to Carey. Beyond this, Carey was lucky to have a wonderful set of friends. There was Bennie the jet- nicknamed after his love of planes especially jumbo jets and of course the Elton John song. Bobby Steele, the strongest kid in school. Beefy Darren, who was equally wide and tall and twice as tall than any of the other boys. Donald Gain, the best quarterback to have on your side when playing football and many more sports. Carey certainly was a popular boy. It all seemed perfect but what Carey needed more than anything was to find himself, he craved it like sugar on strawberries. He knew that there was more to life than the perfect, little bubble that he lived in. He needed to find himself. There was more out there for him and he knew it.

"Everything can seem perfect,

But it's not necessarily worth it.

I have fun times and great friends,

But if I stay the story ends.

I don't want it to stop here,

Not when my dreams are so near.

I can just reach out and grab them,

Life should be a diamond, not a cheap gem.

Yes everything here is pretty fine,

But it's not a life that I want to be mine.

I have so much further to go,

Leaving here is opening the curtains on my show.

I'll tell my friends what they already know,

Then I'll explain why I have to go.

I have so much more to do and be,

There's such a wide world that I must see!"

Carey kept walking until he came to a small bridge over the ravine. He wanted to flow like the tide in that water, fast, clear and right out of the town that he lived in.

He stood for a short while looking at the water rush by with a smile on his face. Closing his eyes he could hear the ripple of waves over the small town traffic. It was a triumph of nature over the noise. He wanted that same feeling so badly to let himself yell out loud and win the day.

While his eyes were shut, he heard another sound. It was the one that made his smile widen and eyes pop open with a glimmer, "That's Bobby's voice. I'd know that voice anywhere!" Carey cried into the wind happily.

He ran towards the sound, letting his feet fall hard on the pavement. In that moment he decided that one day, there would not be the same cold concrete of his hometown under his feet. Instead he would be on the boulevard of the big city. He let his imagination run wild as he ran towards the sound.

When Carey reached Bobby, he imagined that he was running off the edge of a sidewalk in a big city. He pretended that he was experiencing flashing street signs, honking car horns and city people speaking loudly. It was a great dream, one that Carey was determined to turn into a reality.

By the time he arrived, he had been running so fast that when he was slowed down by Bobby, his feet slid in the dirt and a puff of dust engulfed the other boys.

"Hey Carey!" Bobby smiled while coughing. He tapped his friend on the shoulder as he greeted him.

"Good to see you, Bobby!" Carey's heart was beating fast from all of the running. He had been going so fast that his feet had barely touched down on the ground. "I was just going to the park with Beefy." He nodded towards the other boy who was tall and skinny.

Beefy gave a nod of his head. "S'up."

"Great there's three of us! Let's meet Bennie and Donald up at the park and start a game of football!"

The three of them ran as quickly as they could. They ran through the neighborhood with their laughter as they joked and jostled each other drowning out the hum of the suburban setting. The streets were familiar. Their feet fell like clockwork, ticking along the walks with a well-rehearsed rhythm like a metronome. They all knew the streets too well. It should have been familiar and comforting but to Carey it was becoming all too repetitive.

"Five friends played football in the park,

They moved and glided for the ball like a hungry

shark.

But one of them was hungry for something big,

To get famous and out of the small city.

Donald slid all the way along the dirt,

Muddying his jeans and dirtying his shirt.

They laughed, then cheered as he made a touchdown,

Carey knew his friend's could almost make him feel

whole.

They had so much fun playing that game,

And afterwards he told them his choice, it wasn't the

same!

Carey had worried that his friends might be sad,

Or they'd think of him as mean or a bit bad.

But playing that game they were part of a team,

Joined together – stitched at the seam.

So when he told them about his great vision,

All the boys supported his decision!

They played until the sun set on the park,

And went home only when the sky turned dark.

The boys knew that it would be their last game,

Things were never going to be the same!

Carey was destined for a better way,

He was opening a chapter on a brand new day.

All that seemed left was to tell his family,

Carey was back to his imagination sight,

He considered all the ways of how to do it right,

And he headed home excited for dinner that night.

When Carey returned home he sat down for 'family dinner'. The excitement ran through him like electricity in a wire. A fire was burning inside him for the beginning of his dream and he knew that he was close.

"I have to wait until they have eaten. They're going to need all of their strength for the shock. They won't see it coming. I should let them enjoy this wonderful cooking mother had made first. It's my favorite; meatloaf with mashed potatoes. I'll tell them after. I need to fill my stomach too. The excitement is too much!"

The aroma of cooking at home filled the air, twisting and turning until Carey's stomach grumbled. He sat down straightaway and enjoyed every bite. It was mouth-watering and delicious. He had to wonder when he would be able to taste food like this again. He started to imagine all of the foods that he would eat in Hollywood but he kept coming back to the great taste of his mother's cooking.

"You've been very quiet today." Carey's sister teased as she flicked a pea at him across the table. Carey smiled. Even his sister's teasing was putting a bigger and bigger smile on his face.

He imagined what his excitement looked like as it bubbled and boiled up within him. He wondered if it would start with a bright golden spark that balled up in his stomach. Would it sizzle or fizz? Grow slowly or explode? Would it shoot up like a sky rocket? He imagined it pouring out from his mouth in a multitude of colorful fireworks – all reds, golds, browns, greens and blues that sparkled and simmered and filled the kitchen. He thought about the bright sparks coating the walls and showering his family. Then they would catch his excitement too. Excitement was always so infectious. It was like laughter that way. Once one person caught it, then it would dance about the space and everyone would feel it.

"I have something to say." Carey said as he stood up. He cleared his throat and everybody looked in his direction. Even Jackson the dog raised his head from his basket and watched as Carey gave his message in a song. He gave each of them a verse and by the time he was done singing, they were all joining in on the chorus.

"I have been thinking for a very long time,

That I would like a life that feels more mine.

I love you all very dear,

But my life can't start while I am here.

I have a dream I need to follow,

So I'll pack my things and leave tomorrow!

Listen to me dad I love you so,

But we both know that it's time to go.

I have a vision I want you to see,

And I'm so glad you'll be supporting me.

You've always been like my rock,

But now it's time for me to pop.

I want to find myself you will see,

So come and join in this excitement with me!

I have been thinking for a very long time,

That I would like a life that feels more mine.

I love you all very dear,

But my life can't start while I am here.

I have a dream I need to follow,

So I'll pack my things and leave tomorrow!

Next I want to thank you mom,

For everything you've said and done.

You made me believe I could do it.

And I can't just stay here and sit.

My feet are itching to get on my way,

And I'll feel your support every day.

You always wanted the best for me,

You made it so that I could see.

My dreams were waiting on the other side.

So send me off with smiles and pride!

I have been thinking for a very long time,

That I would like a life that feels more mine.

I love you all very dear,

But my life can't start while I am here.

I have a dream I need to follow,

So I'll pack my things and leave tomorrow!

What about you my big sister?

I won't be a boy, I'll be a Mister.

Mister Carey will be my name,

Our lives will never be the same.

Things are good but they'll be great!

I'll make it better, no need to wait.

You will always be close as can be,

I'll miss you as much as our family!

I have been thinking for a very long time,

That I would like a life that feels more mine.

I love you all very dear,

But my life can't start while I am here.

I have a dream that I need to follow,

So I'll pack my things and leave tomorrow!

Last but not least we come to my dog Jackson,

I'll miss you but I need to take action.

I have a life waiting for me.

I'll make it big, just wait and see.

You were a very faithful dog, my friend,

And this is not the journey's end.

This is just the start you know.

I need to water my dreams and let them grow!

I have been thinking for a very long time,

That I would like a life that feels more like mine.

I love you all very dear,

But my life can't start while I am here.

I have a dream I need to follow.

So I'll pack my things and it's time to go!

So family let's sing it one more time,

By now you should remember the rhyme!

I'll be a star, you will see.

So one last chorus, 1, 2, 3!

I have been thinking for a very long time,

That I would like a life that feels more mine.

I love you all very dear,

But my life can't start while I am here.

I have a dream I need to follow,

So I'll pack my things and leave tomorrow!

After the song the room felt lighter. Joy was dancing in the air. Carey's mother hugged him close and when she pulled back held his cheeks. She squeezed and looked into his eyes with pride. She and Carey had the same eyes. They both sparkled brightly with happiness but hers glimmered with joyous tears.

"You must do this my boy! You must follow your dreams." She said.

His father patted him on the shoulder and spoke.

"I am proud of you. You are becoming a man. This trip will turn you from a boy to the man you are meant to be. No matter how far away you go, we will always be here for you."

Carey was so emotional, but he kept his composure and shook his father's hand. He shook it with a firm grasp like a man making a business deal.

Next it was his sister that gave him a tight hug.

"I will miss you! More than you could know. Write to me, won't you?" She begged.

"Of course I will!" Carey laughed. She was hugging him so tightly that he wondered if she had been a constrictor snake in the past life.

There was just one more person to say his goodbye to and it would be the hardest.

As he knelt to Jackson and pat his head, he kept his voice soft.

"Well boy. I wish I could take you for one more walk, but the walk to find myself might be a bit long even for us, and I don't think that they would let you on a bus or train."

Jackson rubbed his head against Carey's hand and gave him an encouraging lick. The boy knew that his dog was wishing him well. They would be reunited again soon.

This is it. My story is about to begin. I have opened the book on the first chapter of my great adventure. I have opened the cover of this book. I read the dedication where I thank my wonderful friends and family and especially my best friend Jackson the dog. The title is set... and now it is time for the big adventure.

There may be some difficult days and there will certainly be lots of hard work, but I know that this story was written for me. It is time to wave goodbye to my loving city and become the hero of my own story. And if I ever struggle then there is a song I can sing.

"This is the start of where I am meant to be,

I am working towards my very own destiny.

At 16 I'll go from a boy to a man,

It may be hard but I know that I can!

When I'm weak my family will help me stand,

All this love will help me achieve what I have planned.

This is the first page in a very long book,

And I can't wait to get a better look.

Tonight I will pack my things in one bag,

And start on the greatest adventure I've ever had!"

Carey slid out the door before the morning sun even hinted at rising. He'd tried his hardest to get some shut eye the night before, but he was far too anxious to even manage a wink. He'd shuffled around his dark bedroom, stuffing things into a backpack with haste. Had he packed a heavy sweater? What about extra socks in case they got wet?

Naturally, Carey's mom couldn't sleep either. The thought of her little boy going out into the big, wide world on his own both terrified, and worried her. She'd slipped a note under his door, hoping not to disturb his packing, to let him know she'd prepared some sandwiches for him to take with him on his journey. It wasn't much, but it would last him until he made it to his destination.

Carey smiled, wandering down the road with only a few dim streetlights to guide his way; he fiddled with a sandwich his mother made, bouncing in the pocket of his hoodie. It was cut in half diagonally, just how he liked it, and double-wrapped in plastic wrap to endure the long trip. He hummed as he walked, trying his best not to overthink. He knew his family would miss him, and he, them, but was it too soon?

A pebble broke the soundlessness in the sky, rustling the birds from the branches to begin their morning songs, as Carey kicked it along. He'd been so fixated on his thoughts, his plans, that he hadn't noticed the sun rising over the horizon.

A car honked, causing Carey to jump to the side with surprise.

"Watch out!" a voice shouted from inside.

"Sorry!" Carey shouted back.

The town was stumbling awake, so he decided to move off the road and onto one of the shortcuts that he and the boys knew all too well. Some led downtown, others to the football field, but this one, would take him right to the railyard.

Carey pushed through the thick brush and across the narrow logs that stretched the creeks and streams; remembering all the times he and his friends would pretend to train jump when the locomotives in the yard would change tracks on the weekends. They talked about skipping town, running away, starting their own bands, and then they'd all laugh together. Of course, none of them were serious, none of them were actually going to just jump on a train and take it as far as it would go. Yet, here Carey was, ready to climb aboard and take one to the end of the line, and the beginning of his new adventure.

Empty cars filled his view as he emerged from the trail. A few cars were being shifted around like usual, nothing uncommon. He climbed through a large hole in the fence, passing by rusted old tankers and halers, admiring the history and their legacy as he weaved along the tracks to the station.

By now, the sun was high, its warmth starting to beam upon his skin and forcing him to roll up the sleeves of his hoodie. The commuters had already made camp on the large, concrete platform, standing as close to the edge as possible without the risk of being nicked by passing trains. They were ready to board the moment the train pulled in, ready to head off to one of the big cities only a short ride away for work.

"Big city..." Carey whispered aloud. This reminded him of his destination; Hollywood. And he knew one of the trains on the line would take him there.

Inside the small station were few old benches for seating, a payphone, a bathroom, and a small kiosk for ticket sales. A few travelers had parked themselves and their luggage on the benches, lit cigarettes dancing between their lips in a choreography of anticipation, leaving the kiosk free for Carey to approach.

The woman behind the glass was aged, tempered by years of joy and adventure that showed with every wrinkle on her face, despite the layers of makeup in an attempt to hide them. The brim of her visor hid the top of her glasses, but the long pearl strands that connected them down to her neck twinkled in the fluorescence of the station lighting. Thick mascara covered thin lashes that adorned heavy lids on honey brown eyes. She barely glanced at Carey as he made his way forward. Just another customer at the beginning of a very long day.

"Ahem," he choked out, trying to calm his nerves.

"Where ya headed?" the ticket lady asked, a cigarette dangling too from her orange-tinted lips.

"Hollywood!" Carey replied with enthusiasm.

"Hollywood? What's in Hollywood for a kid like you?"

"Fame, fortune, maybe even a little romance!"

The woman behind the counter laughed heartily, grasping at a few levers, and punching a ticket before passing it over the counter, "that'll be $74.50, kid."

Carey gasped, "$74.50?"

"Did I stutter? So, have ya got the cash or what?"

"Uh..." Carey paused, "Gimme a minute."

He stepped to the side, letting the next customer in line move past him. He fumbled through his pockets, counting the change and examining the few bills in his wallet. He had cash on him, but it was meant to last a week or two, and that ticket would end up taking most of his savings.

A sense of dread began to wash over Carey, and he began to feel defeated. His journey had barely begun and already a rock had fallen before him. He strolled back out to the platform, watching the commuters as they shuffled aboard the train, ready to be whisked off by a metal container on wheels to another world. He sighed, listening to the whistle blow as the train chugged forward, beginning its journey ahead.

"Train, train, I guess this is it. Train, train, I was a fool, I'll admit."

A voice called out from the shadow of the station's overhang, "why so glum?"

CHAPTER II

GYPSY WOMEN

Carey turned, looking over his shoulder to see a young woman perched on a bench, her body leaning forward and her legs swinging back and forth. She had deep emerald eyes that stared at Carey mysteriously while her thin lips were poised into a devious smile.

"Missed my train," Carey replied, turning to face her fully.

She pushed off her seat, choppy brown hair shifting in the wind just above her shoulders as the train finally pulled away completely. A long dark cloak covered much of her upper torso, black ragged jeans barely peeking beneath a layered skirt made of all sorts of patterned fabrics. Some had crowns, cats, and some were just confusing to look at for too long. Heavy dark brown boots clomped on the hard concrete as she strode toward Carey, her smile growing ever-wider.

"Where ya headed?" she asked on her approach.

"I was going to Hollywood," Carey replied, exasperated.

"Hmm...I think the one back there heads out in about 10 minutes," she said, pointing to one of the larger cargo carriers.

"Really?" Carey perked up, turning to glance at the locomotive.

"Yeah!"

"But... I don't have the money."

"Who said anything about money?"

Carey looked at the girl, puzzled by her proposal. Her deep green eyes flickered with mischief as she grabbed Carey's hand, tugging him along as she scooped her duffle from the bench.

"C'mon!" she shouted, letting go of his hand and jumping down onto the tracks.

"Are you nuts?" Carey cried.

"C'mon. You wanna get to Hollywood dontcha?"

The girl ran off, disappearing behind a car before Carey followed. He felt crazy, but also a little excited as he climbed down the platform and ran after her. He lost sight of her pretty fast, but the sound of her heavy boots digging into the gravel around the tracks kept his directions in order.

"Hey!" he shouted, "I didn't catch your name!"

"It's Nikki!" she shouted from somewhere beyond the maze of train cars and stalled engines.

"Nikki? I'm Carey!"

"It's Nikki Good-bye. Y'know, like aaaaah see you later!"

Her footsteps stopped just as Carey rounded the last corner of a broken-down tanker. He looked back and forth, taking small, quiet steps forward as he tried to find her. He strolled past a cargo container, only a few steps, before he felt a hand on his shoulder. It was Nikki, and she yanked him into the car by the straps of his backpack with all her strength.

Carey took a few moments to catch his breath as he sat in the cargo hold, trying to collect himself from both confusion and fright.

"Shh!" Nikki hushed, pressing a finger to her lips. She hustled them behind a few large crates off to the side that smelled oddly like a mix of hay and tobacco. "If they find us, we're in big trouble."

Carey peeked out from their hiding spot just in time to see a security guard looking inside each car, clearly checking for hitch-hikers, and anything else that looked strange.

A voice grumbled loudly from outside, turning the guard's attention before he closed the door to their car. They listened as his steps moved away from the car just as the train whistle blared out to signify its departure. A few short moments later the train lurched forward, shifting them, and the crates.

"Yikes. Better move, quick," Nikki remarked with a wink.

Carey watched as she jumped over the crates and closer to the back of the car. As he didn't feel like being crushed by boxes of tobacco either, he followed suit, coming to sit just in front of the crates he'd boarded earlier.

"So," Nikki continued, "What's in Hollywood? Friends? Family? Oooh, maybe a girl?"

"Fame," Carey replied, "I'm gonna be famous."

Nikki laughed, leaning back against the wall of the car.

"And where are you going?" Carey asked defensively.

"Me?" Nikki asked, looking at him with a bit of surprise, "I dunno."

"You don't know"

"Wherever the road takes me."

"So, you're some kind of drifter?"

Nikki laughed again, "You're not very street smart are ya?"

Carey frowned.

"They call us Gypsies, y'know? You see 'em at the circus and stuff. Some of 'em use a crystal ball, or a deck of cards. We can read people's futures."

"Can you tell my future?"

"I dunno. I haven't really tried to tell anyone's future before."

"So try me!"

The car shuffled as it moved along the tracks, occasionally slowing to pass another train, or change tracks. Time moved slowly for the duo, but already the day was ending. Carey could feel the chill in the air that came with the setting of the sun.

The pair sat across from one another, cross-legged. Carey placed his hands upon his knees, palm facing upward and Nikki stared down at them with great focus. She carefully analyzed each line on his hands, humming and hawing as she looked them up and down.

Carey stared forward, taking in the sight of Nikki in the fading daylight, her beautiful brown hair, her dimpled cheeks, her curious attire. She smelled faintly of cedarwood and patchouli, reminding him of the little pawn shop downtown he liked to wander into on rainy days.

"So, what do they say?" Carey finally asked.

"Lots of things," Nikki replied.

She traced a line through his left palm, her black-painted nail gently skimming him and almost tickling him, "This one means love, and it's pretty deep which means it's either gonna hit ya soon, or it already has."

Carey gulped.

She traced another line on his right hand, "This one shows a crossroad in the near future. See how it passes over another? It means your path may change, or cross with someone else's to bring about a decision." She continued on before finally tracing one last line down to his wrist, "And this one shows the long road to the fame you're seeking."

"Fame," Carey muttered in response.

Nikki nodded briefly before pulling her hands away and letting out a large yawn.

The two sat opposite one another, discussing where they came from and where they were off to, what they wanted out of life and the road ahead. Carey had pulled out a couple sandwiches from his pack, offering one to Nikki which she quickly snatched up without hesitation. They saw a few flickers of light as they passed a couple of rail-crossings, but they mostly sat in darkness.

"So, what else do you do? I mean, when you're not at the circus," Carey asked. He didn't want to pry, but he really was curious. He'd only been to the circus once, when he was a little boy, and he didn't really remember much beyond the clowns and elephants.

"We travel a lot," Nikki replied. "Some people don't care much for us. Especially not in small towns like yours, so we keep moving. We do readings, cheap card tricks, whatever earns us a couple bucks."

"But you're just a kid too. Don't you have 'family'?"

Nikki's smile faded slightly, "Gypsies are family. Maybe not by blood, but by work."

"So, where's the rest of the Gypsies?"

"I'm not sure. We all got split up on the last route because of a storm. I'm going to find them, Carey. I've gotta find 'em." Nikki said rather matter-of-factly.

Carey nodded, not knowing whether Nikki could see him or not. There was a strength to her words, a strength he knew all too well. He'd held the same tone when he decided to go to Hollywood. Carey then pondered Nikki's reading, wondering how real, and how truthful it really was. Would he really be famous? Was he willing to work for it? And what about that 'love' reading? He looked over, still managing to trace Nikki's silhouette even in the pitch black of the rail car. A strange song began to fill his head, the tune low and slow, but still encompassing his every thought.

(Gypsy Woman you're moving too fast.

Gypsy Woman it ain't gonna last.

Gypsy woman you're moving too fast.

Catch Airra Plane quick before you run out of gas, Gypsy Woman)

He snapped back to reality as the train screeched to a halt.

"This is my stop," Nikki announced, moving to the door and sliding it open with a loud thud.

"Wait," Carey protested.

"What?"

"I, uh..." Carey fumbled, flustered with what to say to convince her not to go just yet. "Come with me!"

"To Hollywood?" Nikki scoffed, "that's not really my thing."

"Why not? You could do readings there for people, it would be a real hit!"

"Bright lights, huge crowds of people..." she trailed off.

"C'mon," Carey begged.

"I'm a Gypsy, Carey. We don't stick around in one place too long."

"I'm not asking you to stay forever. Just long enough for another adventure."

Nikki smiled, "You're very unpredictable, small-town boy."

Carey grinned, stretching out his hand to the emerald eyes peering at him in the faint light of the train station.

"Just this once. One last dance. I'll make it quick and make it last."

Nikki shook her head, "There's a reason they call me Nikki Good-bye," she continued. "I never stay…" And with that, she hopped off the train and into the night.

Carey sat back and grasped at every mild thought that swept passed his mind's eye. He believed that Nikki was not only his way onto the train, and, by proxy, his ticket into a new life. But she was also the propelling force that rocked him out of his comfort zone. Nikki had enough spunk and confidence for the both of them, but now that she was gone.

CHAPTER III

YOUNG DREAMER

Carey couldn't help but revert back to doubting himself. Anxiety plagued him as the very thought of failure consumed him whole. What if he wasn't good enough to find himself? What if no one found him to be as different as he thought he was? What if he got out there into the big city and everything ended up being the same? What if after all this, he turned out to be a joke. A boy with nothing to show for his life but hope and a dying prayer.

In an effort to rid him of the self-pity party he was throwing for himself, he stood and paced until he felt as though the soles of his shoes wear thin. But in the midst of his pacing, the luggage that was stored in the boxcar with him seemed to whisper to him. If Nikki were here, she'd go through them without hesitating simply because she wanted to see what was stored in all those bags. At first, Carey shook his head and kept his hands to himself. He ignored the bags. Ignored the thought of Nikki. He ignored everything as best as he could. But his eyes seemed to constantly find their way to the suitcases. What's the worst that could happen? Nothing in the bags would harm him, but also, going through them wouldn't harm the people that owned the bags. But boredom was starting to drill holes into his skull, so he made a beeline for the biggest suitcase he could find.

Carey ran his fingers across the rough fabric of an oddly colored screen suitcase. When he touched the handle of its zipper, he rubbed it between his index finger and thumb. The coolness of it steadied his thoughts and in turn, calmed his anxiety-riddled heart.

Upon opening the suitcase he found the usual assortment of folded clothes. But none of that interested him. What snagged his attention was a pair of men's leather dress shoes that were the color of baked tangerines. Carey removed the shoes from the mesh lining that they were encased in and rubbed the palms of his hands along the delicate seam that pieced the shoes together. He had never owned a pair of shoes as expensive or pristine or flat out unusual as them before.

"Wouldn't hurt to try them on," he whispered to himself while comparing the size of the shoes against the bottoms of his feet. When he felt confident enough to believe that they'd fit, he kicked off his slightly worn shoes and gently slid his feet into the unusual pair. He gasped not because of how they fit like a glove; but because they looked perfectly at home on his mediocre feet. Carey laced up the shoes and walked around in them while making sure he wasn't seen. But Carey couldn't stop the flood of thoughts that entered his mind. He imagined that he was an A- list actor debuting his new look on the red carpet. He smiled broadly at the thought and then imagined that he was walking into a car dealership and purchased the most expensive shiny thing on the lot. He imagined that he was widely known by hundreds of thousands, if not millions of fans that he would never meet. He imagined signing autographs for them and making women swoon in those loud and obnoxiously delicious shoes. But the reality of his life caught up with his growing imagination, and once again, he felt his anxiety creep up on him and perch on his shoulder. With a sad and defeated sigh, Carey took off the shoes and carefully put them back where he found them. He searched through another suitcase, a burgundy one this time, and was pleasantly surprised by the contents inside. Carey found a pair of sheer pantyhose, a silk navy blouse, a few other skirts and dresses, and a journal with a lock on it. He picked up the pantyhose and slipped his hand into one of the legs to test its sheerness, and then Carey picked up the blouse. It felt like water in his hands as it rippled over and under his fingers. Carey imagined the woman who would wear clothes that dainty and exquisite and believed that she was either someone of importance or someone with fashionable taste. He imagined her to be a tall woman with long, beautifully shaped stems for legs and imagined her to be slender. He pictured this woman to be blonde with bright blue eyes, but liked the imagery of a brunette with short brown hair that curled around her ears, and had the biggest hazel green eyes instead. He took his daydream further and imagined her sitting across from him in one of the boxcars — first class of course — and toyed with the idea of her laughing at something witty that a sophisticated version of himself would say. He imagined her holding a porcelain teacup between her manicured fingers before taking a thoughtful sip of the tea inside. Maybe she'd cross and uncross her legs, but only at the ankle.

Carey raised the blouse to his nose and sniffed. The perfume that lingered there smelled like freshly cut lemons and rosemary. To Carey, the scent was intoxicating. But while folding the blouse and putting it away, Carey realized that a woman who wore clothes like that and smelled like a walking meadow would never look his way. Not if he remained or carried out the rest of his life as a mediocre man. A woman like that, one with virtue and self-respect would only entertain the jokes of a man wearing leather tangerine shoes. Carey frowned while looking down at himself. It wasn't about the clothes or the women, not completely at least. Sure, he wanted fame but ultimately he wanted a better life for himself. He wanted to grow his self-confidence and thrive in his passions. He wanted the respect of others, but deep down within the hollow space in his chest, he wanted to respect himself. The anxiety and fear that once clouded his mind, dulled and dissipated, leaving behind a sense of strength and resolve that he was sure Nikki would've been proud of. With the same surety as the forward moving train, Carey was also determined to surge forward into the life that he knew was within his grasp.

As long as he worked for it, that is.

CHAPTER IV

DON'T WORRY I'LL BE THERE

Carey had fallen into a deep slumber after exploring other interesting-looking luggage in the boxcar. The steady lull and drift of the train had helped ease him to a comfortable snore. But sleep soon made way for ravenous hunger which startled him awake. That along with the sudden noise of the train screeching to a stop.

The drone of evening commuters moving on and off the train, along with the mouthwatering smell of hot food—roasted corn as well as several different street meats: pastrami, roast beef, sausages... Carey knew for sure he was at some in-between station (not his stop), but at least he could get something to eat, if he was careful. His stomach rumbled, pouncing on the idea.

Standing on a crate of tobacco, Carey was able to carefully peer outside the small and only window of the boxcar. And behold he was greeted by a curdle of ground-mist beneath the evening stars. Ahead, a large station flared with white light and a host of people teeming around kiosks for tickets. This wasn't Hollywood, but he was closer… closer to his dreams. His eyes filled with warmth of tears as he watched the oasis of business people in stiff suits walking briskly; blue-collar workers ambling like snails, loud crews of rambunctious men brushing along, families huddled together. A vandal dashed away from a graffitied wall and two overweight security guards sprung after him. Life was happening around Carey. The smell of cheap cologne, cigarette smoke, sweat and hair products-all intermingled - filled his nostrils. The air was thriving and heavy and surprisingly not unpleasant. People were talking, coughing, laughing. Hundreds of people owning their own stories and dreams. The whoosh of an arriving train, its intense yellow headlights and chiming bells made his heart jump with delight. Carey got down from the crate and found his own backpack. He re-buckled it and shouldered it. He felt better and the whistling hole in his gut stopped, for the time being. He felt like himself again.

Not long after, a dog began to bark - the heavy voice bark of a really big fellow just outside his boxcar. Carey froze for a moment.

"Smell something, boy?" The gruff voice of a train conductor accompanied the dog's growl.

Quickly goose bumps spread all over Carey's body as a bolt of terror both sharp and yet undefined struck him.

Suddenly the door of the boxcar flew open.

Carey saw a giant of a man in a dirty uniform and an ugly bulldog rush across toward him. The conductor was brandishing a black iron cane, squinching his bloodshot eyes. *"Get OUT!"* he screeched, and the voice emerging from that huge barrel chest was deadly-it was the voice of many claps of thunder. "Out! You stowaway thief!" He jabbed the cudgel at Carey's stomach. The sudden pain sent him reeling. The conductor reached out - almost casually - and grabbed the boy by the scruff of his neck.

"Please!" Carey wailed, fighting to free himself as the bulldog barked wildly around him. "Let go!"

But the man clamped a very strong hand over the boy's upper arm. "Let's go," he said, half-dragging Carey out of the train, squeezing Carey's arm hard enough to leave bruises. "Bloody stowaway!"

The commuters around them parted to let the conductor through. Some of them grinned sympathetically at Carey.

"You're hurting me!"

"Not as much as I'm *going* to hurt you," the man said and pulled him across the floor. A couple of men—rail workers in orange vest that gave high visibility in dark places —laughed. They had greedy, thoughtless faces. And from the look in their eyes, they were quite used to the conductor torturing stowaway kids.

"Please! You don't understand. Please! I am not a thief!" Carey tried to make his case.

The conductor said "Each *please* is another strapping," then growled, and the men laughed again.

Sensing danger, Carey tried to move but tripped over his own feet and fell into a muddy puddle.

There was a roar of brutal, empty laughter at this—the sort of laughter Carey heard from some of the bigger boys at school, the ones who played hooky and called the younger boys strange but somehow terrifying names.

Carey did not get up but merely lie there on the mud with people passing around him or looking down at him with that mildly sympathetic but disconnected glance of people who are in transit and cannot be bothered.

The conductor shook Carey by the scruff of the neck and looked at him with dark gray melancholy eyes. Carey saw something stirring in those eyes, something deep down. His fear was suddenly sharper, something with a point, jabbing into him. *He's crazy*—this was the intuition which jumped freely into Carey's mind. *"This man is mad"*.

There were two odors about him. The top was what his mother called "all those men's perfumes," meaning after-shave, cologne, whatever. Beneath it, however, was a more vital, even less pleasant smell: it seemed to pulse out at him. It was the smell of sweat in layers and dirt in layers, the smell of a man who bathed seldom, if ever.

Carey's stomach knotted and roiled.

The man tapped Carey lightly on the wrist with his cane. Carey, his nerves screwed up to an unbearable pitch, screamed. Giggling, the man looked coldly at Carey and said something Carey didn't hear.

Violently, the conductor reached out and grasped Carey's muddy arm with one white, spider like hand. He drew Carey toward him, into those smell of old rancid filth. His weird gray eyes peered solemnly into Carey's. The boy felt his bladder grow heavy, and he struggled to keep from wetting his pants. "Who are you?" the man asked.

The words hung in the air over the two of them.

Carey could not quite hide his despair. He could hear the man's dog growling and ready for blood.

Tell me the truth; I will know a lie, this man's eyes said. Tell me the truth or I'll set my dog on you.

And for a moment, everything trembled on Carey's lips: 'Hollywood — I am heading to fame. I want no trouble, sir.'

But Carey made no answer. He knew nothing he would say could save him now. This brute wanted blood, and blood he was going to get.

"Who are you?" the conductor asked again, drawing even closer. And on his face Carey now saw total confidence — he was used to getting the answers he wanted from people . . . and not just from sixteen-year-old kids, either.

Carey took a deep, trembling breath and screamed: "*I AM NOT A THIEF!*"

The conductor, who had been leaning even farther forward in an anticipation of a broken and weak whisper, recoiled as if Carey had suddenly reached out and slapped him. The man lunged forward and pushed Carey in the chest. He fell full-length in the mud, moaning.

A muffled burst of laughter came from the rail workers.

"You simple-minded, snot-nosed brat," the conductor shrieked. His voice was now as high and shrewish as he kicked the boy.

More laughter echoed among the spectating men.

The pain seemed to sink into Carey's flesh, not lessening but actually intensifying. It was hot and maddening. He screamed and writhed in the mud.

"*Bad boy! Bad boy!* Very *bad!*" the man shouted.

Each "bad" was punctuated by another crack of the conductor's cane, another fiery handprint, another scream from Carey. His back was burning. He had no idea how long it might have gone on — the conductor seemed to be working himself into a hotter frenzy with each blow — but then a new voice shouted: "Stop!"

A tall straight man in a neater uniform appeared on the scene. He spoke to the rail workers, and then turned to the mad conductor. There was no more laughing, no more beating. The new man spoke quietly. Carey saw strength and spirit dissipate from his tormentor.

The rail workers shifted on their feet. Their shoulders sank. They began to drift away. The tall man turned to the conductor.

"Sorry, Sir Philip. I got carried away," the brutish conductor blurted and briskly walked away with his bulldog. His voice, petrified and slightly out of breath, came with a squeak.

For the moment while this 'Sir Philip' faced in Carey's direction, in effect 'shooing' the group of men away with his presence, Carey saw a long pale lightning-bolt of a scar zigzagging from beneath his right eye to just above his jawline.

A hand grasped Carey's elbow and helped him to his feet. When he staggered, the arm attached to the hand slipped around his waist and supported him. Carey staggered again. The world kept wanting to swim out of focus. Trying to fight the fear and confusion, Carey gazed at the tall man who had just helped him… probably a senior train worker.

"Are you all right, boy?" Sir Philip whispered.

"Yes… I think so."

"Good." Looking neither to the left nor to the right, Sir Philip departed, weaving his way through the crowd, apparently headed to the train.

"Sir!" Carey yelled, but the man marched on through the slow-moving crowd.

Despite the pain smartening on his back, Carey got to his feet and ran around a group of men and women hauling baggage, shot through a gap between two other bands of people talking on the platform, and finally was close enough to the man to reach out and touch his elbow. "Sir?"

The man wheeled around, freezing where Carey stood. Up close, the scar seemed thick and separate, a living creature riding on the man's face. Even unscarred, Carey thought, this man's face would express a forceful impatience. "What is it, boy?" the man asked.

"Sir, this is all I have. Not enough to buy a ticket." Carey dug into the roomy pocket of his pants and closed his fingers around a few bucks—his life savings—and displayed it on his palm. "Please help me get back home. I'll work for it. Clean floors. Wash restrooms."

When Carey looked up at Sir Philip's face, half-expecting a forceful grab, the conductor merely smiled. The impatience which had seemed so characteristic had utterly vanished. Softness momentarily distorted the man's strong features. He lifted his hand to Carey's, and the boy thought he meant to take the money: he would have given it to him, but the man simply folded the boy's fingers over the dollar bills on his palm. "Follow me," he said.

They went towards the side of the train, and Sir Philip led the way. In the glowing darkness of the night, the man's face looked as though someone had drawn on it with thick pink crayon. "What did you steal?" he asked calmly enough.

"I swear I didn't steal anything."

The man shook his head. "I don't believe you."

"I'm telling the truth," Carey said. "I didn't steal anything." Tears streamed down his eyes. "I just wanted to get to Hollywood. I met this gypsy lady at the station and she took me aboard."

'Sir Philip' shook his head. "Describe this gypsy lady. I'm going to find out if you're lying right now, boy, so I'd make this good if I were you."

"She's young," Carey said. "Green eyes, brown hair." He thought he saw recognition of some kind of flash in the man's eyes. "She dresses funny — wears a cloak."

Seemingly satisfied with the boy's description, the man nodded and ushered Carey into one of the sleeping cars of the train. Walking down a quiet hallway, they quietly emerged into a small room with one bed and one wooden chair. The man cocked his head to one side and considered Carey for a long moment, worry very plain upon his face. "Now you must answer a question of mine," he said.

"Yes."

"How bad do you want it, boy?"

"Want what?"

"How bad do you want to learn who you are?"

Carey closed his eyes, his bones aching with pain from the beating, and shook his head. "I don't know anymore."

The man smiled. There was no humor in that smile. A muscle just below the eye on the unscarred cheekbone jumped like a fish. He pressed his hands together, palm to palm. "Why don't you know?"

Carey could practically feel the man vibrating, controlling his growing agitation only from a lifetime's habit of self-discipline.

"I'm not cut out for this. I don't think I'm strong enough."

The man appeared not to have heard Carey's answer. He was looking away into the corner of the room as if there was something there to see. He was thinking long and hard and fast; Carey recognized that. And his father had taught him that interrupting an adult who was thinking hard was just as impolite as interrupting an adult who was speaking. But—

Carey looked at the man, who was now staring at him with his lips drawn back from his teeth all the way to the gum lines. The man nodded and began to speak.

"Now listen to me. I won't stop you from returning back home. But I've worked this train for three decades and I've seen many runaway kids just like yourself hitchhike with the promise of something better." He shifted away from the boy with a military smoothness, looking out the window.

"I see them come on this train with big dreams like yours—either running from something or running to something. Most of them never make it. They see the unforgiving harshness of the real world and they run back home, which is not a bad thing. Some fall by the wayside. Sadly."

Suddenly tears came in a hot and burning flood for Carey.

"But I know you're special, Carey," the man said, and surprised Carey by winking at him. "I see a light in you that I've not seen in anyone for a long time. See. I'll make a deal with you. Keep going to your destination. Go to your dream. And if it's not what you expected, you can always come back to this train because I'll always be here. You think you can do it? Convince yourself to give it a try?"

Carey whispered something.

"What?" Sir Phillip asked sharply.

"I said I don't want to go," Carey said, only a little louder. Tears were close and he knew that once they began to fall he was going to lose it. Just blow his cool entirely.

"I think it's too late for you to give up," Sir Phillip said. "I don't know your tale boy, and I don't want to. I didn't even want to know your name. But I know you're special."

Carey stood looking at him, shoulders slumped, eyes burning, his lips trembling.

"Get your shoulders up!" Sir Phillip shouted at him with sudden fury. "Now listen and I'll give you some advice. You can't cry off, boy. You're too young to be a man, but you can at least *pretend*, can't you? You look like a kicked dog!"

Stung, Carey straightened his shoulders and blinked his tears back.

"Better," Sir Phillip said dryly. "Not much, but a little. The train leaves in five. Make up your mind." Then he walked out of the room abruptly.

His clothes and skin packed with mud, Carey sat on the wooden chair. It creaked as it took on his weight. The loneliness and homesickness rose in him again. Carey couldn't fight them off. For minutes later, drooping with weariness and hungry again, which was somehow worse, he locked the door behind him, but it didn't make him feel any safer. He stripped to the skin, not liking the feel of his clammy, muddy clothes.

He pulled out fresh clothes from his backpack, thinking he would put the dirty ones in his pack in the morning -they would be dry then-and perhaps clean them along the way, maybe in a Laundromat, maybe just in a handy stream.

While looking for socks, his hand touched something slender. Carey pulled it out and saw it was his toothbrush. Immediately, visions of home and warmness - everything a toothbrush could embody - welled up and overcame him. The emotions rushed inside him like a flood. A toothbrush was a thing to be found in a well-lit bathroom, a thing to be used with warm slippers on the feet and cotton pajamas on the skin. It was nothing to find in the bottom of your backpack in a freezing, dark place.

Loneliness erupted through him; his strong resolve breaking piece by piece. Carey began to weep. He did not cry screamingly or scream as people do when they cover anger with tears; he wept in the stable sobs of one who has seen just how alone he is and likely to continue for a long time. He sobbed because all reason and safety appeared to have fled his world. Loneliness was here, a powerful reality.

Carey wanted to be so determined that nothing can take him down no matter how hard it tries to. A guard glazed over the contents of the back car and slammed the car door shut. "All clear!" the man hollered, heading back into the train station where a number of people were waiting to board. Some were munching, some were gossiping on the phone, some were even sleeping with a bit of drool spilling from the corner of their mouths. A stressed looking mother with a few wrinkles on her cheeks was bouncing an unhappy baby on her hip. From the car, Carey could hear the baby wailing like it had been beaten brutally. Unbeknownst to him, the baby was extremely fussy from a long day of traveling that wasn't even halfway done yet.

The train whistle sounded, ringing in Carey's ears and causing great stress to his eardrums. The train jolted forward, departing from the stressful scene back at the station straight for the place where all of Carey's dreams would come true. It was so dark outside that Carey could hardly see his hands in front of him. It was also beginning to get chilly. Thankfully, Carey had packed a heavy sweater because he knew his mother would worry if he hadn't packed it. Because the train was keeping a steady enough pace for Carey to move around without being tossed across the cart, he stood up and retrieved a baby blue sweater that was so thick it made your arms feel heavy. *Thanks Mom,* Carey thought to himself as he leaned his back against the side of the car for support. Soon, his eyelids became heavier and heavier until he was unable to keep them up and Carey fell asleep before the tears had entirely run their course. He slept curled around his backpack, almost naked except for the blue sweater, clean underpants and socks. The tears had cut clean courses down his dirty cheeks, and he held his toothbrush loosely in one hand.

The train came to a screeching halt, ripping Carey away from his peaceful slumber. The sun was shining down on his eyes, causing him to squint so hard that creases formed around his eyes. Its whistle blew loudly, once again ringing in his ears. He sat up. Stunned.

He was still in the box car that he and Nikki jumped on. He had fallen asleep in that box car and stayed asleep. His clothes were clean. He saw no mud. He felt no bruises on his back from the conductor's cane, no laughing train workers and no Sir Philip. "A dream. That was all a dream. Why?"

There came the sound of a dog barking outside the car.

"You smell something boy?"

Carey swallowed hard. The door started to open. Then stopped.

The guard got a call.

"You got a freeloader? Where?"

The guard left the door slightly ajar as he moved with excitement towards his associates' call.

Carey exhaled.

Feedback from the intercom screeching on the distant platform could be heard. "Passengers departing from Los Angeles, please hold until the train has been confirmed empty. I repeat, passengers departing from Los Angeles, please hold until the train has been confirmed empty. Thank you." In this moment, Carey could have sworn his heart stopped right there. He glanced through the crack in the door, up to see the large sign (California). "I made it...I made it to California!" Carey sat with his bag pressed against his chest staring in awe. It was almost unreal to him. Soon, all of his dreams were going to come true. He would be famous, everybody would know his name, young children would want to be him.

I can just hear the crowd going wild already. "Carey! Carey! Carey!" The sound of a wild and large crowd echoed in his mind and bounced off his ear drums until the sound of the distant passenger train doors opening snatched him out of his trance. Suddenly, it struck him that he needed to safely get off the train. *If only I had Nikki here with me to guide me off this train properly.* Through the wall, Carey could hear hundreds of people exiting the train. They were people of all origins and backgrounds. Even young toddlers were hopping down the steps and excitedly taking their first step in California. He scanned through the door to see further to the left two beefy security guards dressed in blue and black with midnight black caps on. They stood with their thumbs in the belt loop of their pants and they seemed to be staring at the crowd in sync searching for freeloaders. *Now is my chance.*

To keep from being seen by the guards, Carey jumped from the box car, joining the crowd quickly, turning his back towards the California sign and slowly scooted backwards on his butt, clutching his bag tightly, until his back hit the large suitcase of a big man in a hurry. Carey was thrown forward. He landed face first just centimeters away from the metal track on the road. He was treated with a mouth full of dirt and a whole lot of throbbing at the top of his head. "Agh.." he groaned, disappointed that his bag didn't break his fall in the slightest. After spitting at the ground until he felt all the dirt was gone, or swallowed, he pressed the palms of his hands into the ground and pushed himself up on his feet. He swept up his bag, and quickly ran until he made it to the front of the train. The awful, screeching feedback from earlier sounded again and the woman was back for another announcement. "Those leaving Los Angeles, you may now board the train. Be sure that your tickets are visible during your time of boarding." This was Carey's chance to walk around the train and leave the station without being seen. He walked around to the front of the train and saw a bunch of people scrambling frantically. There were so many different changes in direction that if Carey inserted himself into the situation, not a soul would notice. This is exactly what he was hoping for. He ran into the crowd, tossing his backpack over one of his shoulders, and he instantly mixed up in the chaos. Not a single person took notice of him, and just like that he was leaving through the open gates that took him away from the train station. The air was warm and there were morning birds chirping, which meant it couldn't have been later than 10 a.m. Just across the street, there was a tall woman wearing a yellow sundress walking her dog. The dog was fluffy and white, panting with its tongue out having a happy life. What reason would the dog have to be unhappy?

It's in California. Carey held his arms out like he was preparing to soar in the sky with the chirping birds and let out a happy sigh. *I can't even decide what to do first...there's so much I've got to do! So many things that I must see! Why...I'm so excited I can hardly breathe.* Carey's heart was pounding in the best of ways. His dreams seemed to be just a few steps out in front of him. All he had to do was reach out his hands and wiggle his fingertips and the fame would tickle him and rush straight through his veins. Or so, that's how he imagined the process to be. "Have you got nothing better to do than stand right in the way of the entrance you bloody idiot?" A man with an accent said with malice, narrowing his eyes at Carey like he had stolen candy from a baby or something.

"Sorry sir, it's just that I'm so thrilled to be in California!" The man stopped walking and turned back towards Carey who was grinning from ear to ear. His eyes were beaming with excitement like a child on Christmas day. "I could care less, do everyone a favor and *move*." Carey's smile faded slightly as the man stomped off, holding one single briefcase with a tight grip. "He's not very nice…" Still, Carey slid to the left so he was no longer blocking the station entrance. He then realized he had no map of Hollywood and really didn't know where he was going to start.

CHAPTER V

WAX MUSEUM

A woman with light brown skin and hip hugging box braids walked through the gate carrying a baby with curly hair on her hip and holding the hand of a walking toddler that looked exactly like the baby but with longer, curlier hair. "Uh, um excuse me ma'am?" The lady turned to look at Carey and tightened her grip on her child's hand. "Yes?"

"Do you happen to know where I can go to achieve my dreams?" The woman's lips curved into a smile and she chuckled from the back of her throat. "What's funny, is there something on my face?"

"Wait...you were being serious about the whole dream thing?" Carey smiled and tucked his thumbs under the straps of his bags.

"Well, why wouldn't I be serious about it?" The woman's baby began to put up a fuss, so she started to bounce the child around on her hip a bit. She sighed.

"I'm not really sure why you came here without a game plan, young man.

She started thinking. "I know somebody, she coaches kids like you.

It'll be a tall, beige looking house with a neon green door right around the corner. Knock on the door three times and ask for Deloris. Tell her that Aleeyah sent you." "Are you Aleeyah?" She furrowed her eyebrows.

"Who else would I be?" Aaleeyah pulled her child's arm as she tried to roam away. "I hope that at least gets you somewhere, young man."

"Thank you so much, Miss. Aleeyah! You have no idea how much this means to me. I won't let you down, everybody 's gonna know my name soon!" Aleeyah stood a while without saying anything. In that time, Carey began to scan her further. Her lips were full and they were tinted with a bold red color. She wore a pair of tan trousers with a white blouse that looked as though it was recently ironed. How she was able to survive a long train ride was beyond Carey, but he didn't spend much time thinking about it before Aaleeyah finally opened her mouth to speak. "Actually, I've got some time to kill. I'll walk you there." Carey's eyes grew to the exact size of dinner plates, popping like popcorn

"Really? Thanks Miss. Aleeyah!"

"Just call me Aleeyah, I ain't old." She stepped ahead of him and motioned for him to come with her to cross the street. "Tameka, make sure you keep up baby. We're about to cross the street." Aleeyah said to the toddler.

The toddler huffed but complied as the three of them rushed across the street as soon as the traffic died down. Once they made it across the street, they headed in the same direction that the lady who was walking her dog was headed. "So boy, what's your name?" Her daughter turned around and looked up at Carey with big, brown eyes.

"Mama, who's this?"

"*Tameka!*" Aleeyah snatched Tameka up and said. "I did not raise you to speak to strangers that way, apologize *now*." Tameka hesitantly spun back around, her eyes threatening tears. "Sowwy." Carey's heart tore a tad bit when he heard the girl's broken voice. The comment hadn't even bothered Carey. She's only a young child after all, no older than four.

"I-I'm Carey. Carey"

"Hi, Carey." said Tameka, her voice still shaky. She still broke into a smile at the thought of meeting a new person. That was just how her soul was as a young human being who hasn't been introduced to the hardships of this world yet. In a way, Carey was similar to her but rather in the sense that he felt he could take anything the world throws at him and can politely give it back in the form of his talent.

"How old are you?" Aleeyah asked.

She turned left on a corner and Carey followed closely behind. "Sixteen." Aaleeyah stopped dead in her tracks and swung around faster than a cheetah could make it around the block.

"What's a young man like you doing out here in California all alone, huh?

Where are your parents?"

"They're back in Ohio."

"And how come y'all didn't travel together?"

"Well...because it's my dream and we're not all that rich to afford four train tickets to California." Aleeyah sighed and continued walking.

"Baby, if you were Tameka or little Darryl, you would still be up in Chicago going to High School and living with me. It's a whole lot of sick people and tricksters in this world and I don't think you're quite old enough to understand all of that."

Carey sighed.

"I know you mean well Aleeyah, but this is my dream. Nothing can get in the way of it, not any sick person or tricksters. I'm old enough to know that this is what I want to do with my life and this is where I need to do it. My hometown doesn't offer me the same resources that

California does. I mean look at me, I'm meeting new people already. This would *never* happen in Ohio."

In her mind, Aaleeyah so badly wanted to keep trying to explain to Carey why traveling alone at such a young age was a bad idea, but she knew that his determination would win the argument so she didn't even bother.

"Mama, where we goin?"

"We're going to Mommy's house for a little while."

Carey arched one of his brows, but figured it was best to stay out of grown folk's business.

"Yay! Is Mommy gonna make us those treats again?"

"Maybe if you ask nicely." Aleeyah stopped in front of a beige building with the neon green door. She described it to a 'T'. "Alright Tameka, why don't you go knock on the door and tell Mommy that Mama is out here."

"Okay, Mama!" Tameka let go of Aleeyah's hands and rushed to the door. With her little hands balled up in fists she pounded on the door as loudly as any toddler could.

"We're going through a rough patch.

Stop making that face at me." Aleeyah stated as though she read Carey's mind. The door opened and standing on the other side was a dark skin woman wearing a long pink dress. She wore a big, bright smile on her face.

"Hello, Deloris!"

The woman, known as Deloris, swept Tameka off her feet and swung her around. Finally, she put Tameka down and glanced at Aleeyah.

"She's getting much better, Lee."

"I'm aware." Aleeyah replied dryly.

The tone in her voice made Carey uncomfortable as it was very apparent that they weren't on the best of terms. "Deloris, this is Carey, he is sixteen years old and has travelled different places trying to find himself. I figured I'd drop him off along with the kids."

"Hello," Deloris said, extending her hand for a handshake.

Carey eagerly approached her and shook her hand with a lot of enthusiasm.

"Nice to meet you Carey."

"I am *so* pleased to meet you, Miss. Deloris!"

Deloris nodded, studying Carey for a moment. "Carey, where are your parents?"

Carey scratched at his neck awkwardly and was about to reply but was cut off by Aleeyah. "They are not with him. They allowed him to travel alone to achieve his dreams." Deloris shot Aleeyah a look of irritation clearly showing behind her eyes. She crossed her arms and said, "He can talk, can't he?'

"Carey, could you take Tameka in the house for me. I would like a moment to speak with Aleeyah." Carey shifted his eyes and shrugged.

"Uh..c'mon Tameka."

"Okay!" Tameka grabbed at Carey's free hand and swung her other arm excitedly.

"Take her to the living room, please. I'll be right with you." Carey entered the house with the children and closed the front door behind him to give them privacy. "The living room is that way, Carey!" Tameka screeched, pointing to a doorway to the right. Carey walked through the doorway and gasped, feeling Tameka's hand slip from his grip. There were two leather couches each leaned up against red painted walls. There were numerous movie covers hanging up on the wall from edge to edge. Carey felt as though he was in Heaven. Tameka plopped down on one of the couches and reached for the TV remote resting on an all glass coffee table. There were numerous magazines with Deloris' name on it and every word about her seemed to be positive. Deloris Shaw, most notable acting coach in all of Hollywood? Flip to page 7 to find out! The lovely Mrs. Deloris Shaw with her biggest success, Jodie Gonzales!

The list of positive things that Deloris had accomplished made Carey feel like Aleeyah couldn't have put him in better hands.

"I can't believe I'm at the home of one of Hollywood's finest acting coaches! I've got to call my mom!" Carey thought to himself, plopping down on the couch beside Tameka.

The front door swung open and slammed shut just as quickly as it was opened. Deloris walked into the living room and told Tameka to, 'go into the kitchen and find those treats your like'. Tameka ran like she was being chased by wolves, she loved those treats. Deloris looked over at Carey and smiled. Welcome to Hollywood. You can use the room upstairs until we figure out a place for you to stay."

"You know your journey doesn't get any easier from here on out don't you? "There are all kinds of people here, some real and some fake as if they were in the wax museum. Folks are going to try to hurt you. But you're lucky today. You've made your first friend today. I'm a friend.

Carey is sobered by the tone in Deloris' voice. "But one thing is for sure. You'll never love yourself more than you will from this moment on just for having the courage to live your dreams."

"I believe in my dreams."

"I know you do. I can see it in your eyes. I see a lot in your eyes and one thing I must tell you as she points to his chest. You don't have to travel very far to find out who you are. Just look inside yourself and find the inner star that makes you happy, and then be that star all the time".

She smiles and says "You did not have to leave home to be that shining star; you were already that shining star right in your own home".

"This is the start of where I am meant to be,

I am working towards my very own destiny.

At 16 I'll go from a boy to a man,

It may be hard but I know that I can.

When I am weak, my new friends will help me stand,

This is not like home and I'll need to be strong,

But I feel a growing inner guide here to keep me from

wrong.

All this love will help me achieve what I have planned,

And the pain that come's will make me a man.

This is the first page in a very long book.

And I can't wait to get a better look,

Tonight I'll unpack my things, my one little bag,

And start on the greatest adventure I've ever had!"